ABOUT THE BANK STR

Seventy years of educatic
teaching have given the Bank Street College of Education
the reputation as America's most trusted name in early
childhood education.

Because no two children are exactly alike in their
development, we have designed the *Bank Street
Ready-to-Read* series in three levels to accommodate the
individual stages of reading readiness of children ages
four through eight.

- ○ *Level 1:* GETTING READY TO READ—read-alouds
  for children who are taking their first steps
  toward reading.
- ● *Level 2:* READING TOGETHER—for children who
  are just beginning to read by themselves but
  may need a little help.
- ○ *Level 3:* I CAN READ IT MYSELF—for children
  who can read independently.

Our three levels make it easy to select the books most
appropriate for a child's development and enable
him or her to grow with the series step by step. The *Bank
Street Ready-to-Read* books also overlap and reinforce
each other, further encouraging the reading process.

We feel that making reading fun and enjoyable is the
single most important thing that you can do to help children
become good readers. And we hope you'll be a part
of Bank Street's long tradition of learning through sharing.

The Bank Street College of Education

To Fred
— B.B.

GOOD NEWS

A Bantam Little Rooster Book
Simultaneous paper-over-board and trade paper editions / June 1991

Little Rooster is a trademark of Bantam Books,
a division of Bantam Doubleday Dell Publishing Group, Inc.

Series graphic design by Alex Jay/Studio J
Associate Editor: Gillian Bucky

Special thanks to James A. Levine, Betsy Gould,
and Erin B. Gathrid.

Library of Congress Cataloging-in-Publication Data

Brenner, Barbara.
Good news / by Barbara Brenner;
illustrated by Kate Duke.

p.   cm.—*(Bank Street ready-to-read)*
"A Byron Preiss book."
"A Bantam little rooster book."
Summary: As the news of Canada Goose's newly
laid eggs spreads from animal to animal, the facts
become monstrously distorted.
ISBN 0-553-07091-6.—ISBN 0-553-35209-1 (pbk.)
[1. Gossip—Fiction. 2. Canada goose—Fiction. 3. Animals—
Fiction.] I. Duke, Kate, ill. II. Title. III. Series.
PZ7.B7518Gn 1991
[E]—dc20

90-31816   CIP   AC

Published simultaneously in the United States and Canada

Bantam Books are published by Bantam Books, a division of Bantam Doubleday
Dell Publishing Group, Inc. Its trademark, consisting of the words "Bantam Books"
and the portrayal of a rooster, is Registered in U.S. Patent and Trademark Office
and in other countries. Marca Registrada. Bantam Books, 666 Fifth Avenue, New
York, New York 10103.

PRINTED IN THE UNITED STATES OF AMERICA

0 9 8 7 6 5 4

Bank Street Ready-to-Read™

Good News

by Barbara Brenner
Illustrated by Kate Duke

A Byron Preiss Book

A BANTAM LITTLE ROOSTER BOOK
NEW YORK · TORONTO · LONDON · SYDNEY · AUCKLAND

It was a sunny spring day.
Canada Goose was sitting
beside the pond.

She saw Wood Duck in the water.
"Wood Duck! I have good news!"
she called.

"Let's hear it," said Wood Duck.

"I've laid four eggs,"
said Canada Goose.

"That *is* good news,"
said Wood Duck.
"I must go and tell Green Frog."

Wood Duck found Green Frog.
"Green Frog, I have good news,"
said Wood Duck.
"Let's hear it," said Green Frog.

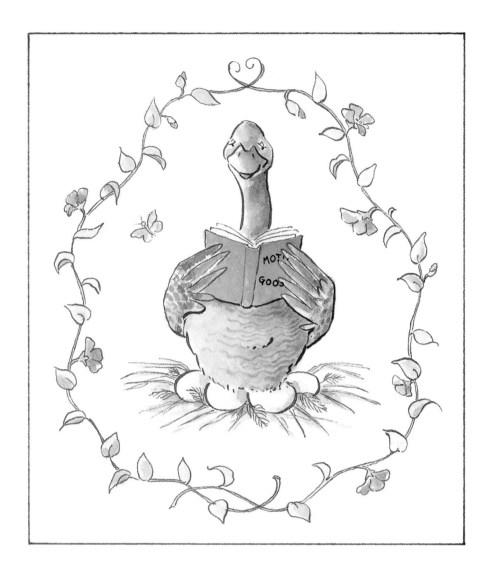

"Canada Goose has laid four eggs.
She is sitting on them."
"That *is* good news,"
said Green Frog.
"We must go and tell Beaver."

They found Beaver.
"Beaver, we have good news,"
Green Frog said.
"Let's hear it," said Beaver.

"Canada Goose is sitting
on five big eggs," said Green Frog.
"Soon they will hatch."
"That *is* good news,"
said Beaver.
"We must tell Mud Turtle."

They found him sleeping.
"Wake up, Mud Turtle,"
Beaver called.
"We have good news!"
"Let's hear it," said Mud Turtle.

"Canada Goose is sitting
on six huge eggs," said Beaver.
"They will hatch any day!"
"That *is* good news,"
said Mud Turtle.
"We must tell Water Snake."

Wood Duck, Green Frog, Beaver, and Mud Turtle
swam off and found Water Snake.

"Water Snake, we have
good news!" said Mud Turtle.
"Let's hear it," said Water Snake.

"Canada Goose is sitting
on seven monster eggs,"
said Mud Turtle.
"They will hatch any minute!"

"That *is* news," said Water Snake.
"But is it *good* news?
We had better go find Muskrat."

They found Muskrat eating.
"Muskrat! We have news!"
called Water Snake.
Before Muskrat could say
anything, Water Snake said,
"Canada Goose is sitting
on eight monster eggs.

And they're about to hatch!"

"That's *bad* news," said Muskrat.
"Monsters hatch from
monster eggs!
Does Canada Goose know that?"

"I don't think so,"
said Wood Duck.
"Then we must tell her,"
said Muskrat.
He jumped into the pond with
Water Snake, Mud Turtle,
Beaver, Green Frog,
and Wood Duck.

They rushed over to Canada Goose.
"Good news!" she called.
"They've all hatched!"

"That's terrible!" said Muskrat.
"No. It's wonderful!"
said Canada Goose.

"Are they big and ugly?"
asked Water Snake.

"No. They're little and cute,"
said Canada Goose.

"Are they really monsters?"
asked Mud Turtle.
"Well, maybe sometimes,"
said Canada Goose.
"But mostly they're my
little darlings."

And she stood up
so they could see.

The animals looked
into the nest.

At last Wood Duck spoke.

"To think," he said,
"that four cute baby geese
could hatch from
eight monster eggs!"